The Shelter Puppy

Other titles by Holly Webb

The Hounds of Penhallow Hall:

Winter Stories:

Animal Stories:

The Shelter Puppy

Holly Webb

Illustrated by Sophy Williams

stripes

For everyone who works with rescued greyhounds –
you are wonderful!

www.hollywebbanimalstories.com

STRIPES PUBLISHING
An imprint of the Little Tiger Group
1 Coda Studios, 189 Munster Road,
London SW6 6AW

A paperback original
First published in Great Britain in 2018

ISBN: 978-1-84715-923-6

A CIP catalogue record for this book is available
from the British Library.

Printed and bound in the UK.

10 9 8 7 6 5 4 3 2 1

Chapter One

Caitlin twirled the end of her ponytail around her finger and tugged at it. She always did that when she was worried. Everyone else in class sounded really excited about coming up with ideas for a charity for her school's Community Week, but she wasn't. She couldn't think of *anything*. Her friend Lily was so enthusiastic she was waving her hands around and talking so fast Caitlin could hardly understand the words.

"The stables where I go riding! We could help them! They're part of this Riding for the Disabled charity, loads of people go there. I even helped last week, it was brilliant! Sometimes it's children who are usually in a wheelchair, but they give them special saddles and it's so amazing to watch. It even seems like the horses know to be careful."

Caitlin nodded. That did sound pretty amazing. In fact, it was obviously a fabulous idea. She gave a tiny sigh. Everyone had been asked to think of a charity that the school might like to support. They were

6

supposed to find out about the charity as their homework over the next two weekends and present the idea to their class. Then each class would vote for their favourite and the staff would pick the final choice. But that meant *she* had to think of a charity and she didn't know where to start.

Of course she'd heard of the RSPCA and Guide Dogs for the Blind. But James who sat on the next table was already talking about guide dogs, and how his next-door neighbours looked after guide dog puppies and they had to learn that they weren't allowed to chase his cat. So that was no good...

Caitlin smiled and nodded at Lily, but she wasn't actually listening to her

friend going on about the ponies at
the riding school any more. She was
thinking about having to stand up
in front of the class and talk. Caitlin
wasn't looking forward to it one bit.
She didn't like people staring at her.
Miss Lewis was always telling her she
had to talk more in class, but Caitlin
tried her best not to. What if she said
something silly and everyone laughed?

Caitlin glanced around – everyone was talking at once and the classroom was buzzing. It was as if every single person there had an idea, except for her. Even Sam Marsh, who never did any homework and had pretended that he had a sprained wrist and couldn't write for two whole days last week, was bouncing up and down in his chair. He was telling all his mates about his fantastic plan. It was something to do with the charity his football club supported, which sent footballs and sports equipment to children in Africa.

Miss Lewis was having a very serious-sounding talk with Amy and Tayla about the hospice where Amy's gran was being looked after and where Tayla's mum worked as a nurse, saying of course they could do it together.

Maybe she could share Lily's riding charity, Caitlin wondered. But that wouldn't really be fair – it was Lily's idea.

"So what do you think you'll do?" Lily asked, finally running out of clever ponies to tell Caitlin about.

"I don't know yet…" Caitlin murmured vaguely. "I suppose I'll think of something. Maybe an animal charity?"

Lily nodded enthusiastically. "I read about a donkey sanctuary in my animals magazine. You could choose that."

"Mm." Caitlin looked down, fiddling with the pencils on the table in front of her. She *did* like the sound of the donkey sanctuary, but she really wanted to think of something for herself.

"Why have you got the car?" Caitlin looked at her mum in surprise. They usually walked home from school – it only took about fifteen minutes and it wasn't as if it was raining.

Caitlin's mum rolled her eyes, but she was smiling. "I can't believe you've forgotten! We're going to see Alice and Sean's new kitten, remember?"

"Oh!" Caitlin brightened up. She had completely forgotten. Mum had told her at breakfast, but worrying about the charity thing at school had sent it right out of her head.

Alice and Sean were her cousins, and they had just got a gorgeous kitten. Mum had shown Caitlin the photos that Auntie Jen had sent, of a black and white kitten curled up on Alice's lap. He was incredibly cute.

Caitlin sped up, hurrying to the car. Auntie Jen had said that the kitten was friendly too, and she was hoping that she would be able to cuddle him.

Her cousin Sean answered the door, with the kitten clinging for dear life on to the shoulder of his school jumper. He was the same age as Caitlin, but he went to a different school, closer to their house. "Hi, Caitlin. Hi, Auntie Sam! Look, this is Ollie."

"Awww! He's so sweet…" Caitlin said admiringly.

"I think he's trying to get out into the garden, Sean," Caitlin's mum pointed out, as the kitten started to scramble down the front of Sean's jumper. "Shall we come in and shut the door?"

Sean scooped up the kitten and snuggled him. "Yes, quick! He tries to get everywhere – he's so nosy. He'd love to get out the front of the house, but he's not allowed yet."

Caitlin's mum closed the door hurriedly and the kitten peered curiously at Caitlin around Sean's hands. His eyes were golden yellow and very round.

"Can I stroke him?" Caitlin asked hopefully, and Sean nodded.

"Sure. He's really friendly." Sean moved his fingers so that Caitlin could pet the black and white kitten, and Caitlin rubbed gently around his silky ears and tickled under his white chin.

"He's so soft!" she whispered delightedly as the kitten stretched out his neck, pointing his nose up to the ceiling and closing his eyes.

"He loves being scratched under the chin," Sean said. "He'll sit for ages if you do that."

Sean's little sister came bouncing down the stairs to hug Caitlin. "Have you seen our kitten?" she demanded excitedly, and Sean sighed.

"Of course she has! She's stroking him right now!"

Alice stuck out her lip and Caitlin broke in hurriedly. She loved being at Alice and Sean's house, but sometimes she went home feeling quite glad that her brother was so much older than she was. It meant they didn't fight nearly as often as Alice and Sean. It was embarrassing when Auntie Jen had to tell her cousins off.

"I love Ollie, he's really cute," said Caitlin, trying to distract the pair of them. "Has he got any cat toys? Can we play with them?" she asked Alice, and her little cousin grabbed her hand and pulled her into the kitchen. Sean came after them with Ollie.

"This is his favourite! It's got

catnip in it." Alice picked up a tiny stuffed mouse with a long tail made of feathers, and Ollie wriggled wildly in Sean's arms, eager to get to the mouse.

It was while they were eating tea (with Ollie trying to climb up everyone's legs to get to the fish fingers, and Caitlin, Sean and Alice all feeding him bits when Caitlin's mum and Auntie Jen weren't looking) that Caitlin had her brilliant idea.

"Where did you get Ollie from?" Mum asked Auntie Jen. "Was it an ad in the newsagent's or something?"

Auntie Jen shook her head. "No, we went to the animal shelter. The one next to Garland Park – you know where I mean?"

"Oh! I thought they only took in dogs."

"No, cats as well. They even had some guinea pigs. I don't think they usually have them, but someone left them outside the shelter and they couldn't find anywhere else to take them."

"They were so sweet!" Alice put in. "They made this little noise like *eeeep, eeeep*!"

"We loved the dogs too, but with

17

me working we simply can't have one. Ollie won't mind having the house to himself for some of the day and it won't be long before he can go outside – we're going to put in a cat flap for him." Auntie Jen sighed. "The shelter manager was telling me that they're struggling at the moment, actually – they're swamped with abandoned dogs that their owners couldn't look after. And the shelter's full all the time. They'd really like to build some more dog pens on the back, but they can't afford it. They need to do some fundraising – not that they don't do a lot already. Extra fundraising, I mean. I thought I might offer to help them run a jumble sale, or something. Maybe a sponsored walk?"

Caitlin let out a squeak of excitement and Auntie Jen leaned over worriedly. "Caitlin, what's the matter, petal? Did your dinner go down the wrong way?"

Caitlin beamed at her. "Nothing's the matter. In fact, everything's perfect!"

The puppy leaped up hopefully, scrabbling at the wire. One of the girls who brought the food had walked past the door of the pen. It wasn't that he was hungry – he'd been fed and he'd even left some of his dinner. He just wanted … somebody.

He wanted somebody to pull on

the other end of his rope toy or race him up and down the yard. Or maybe somebody to squabble with about who got to have the best ball. And then he wanted somebody to snuggle up with in his basket. It was too big for him all on his own, even with the old Winston bear and the scruffy blanket.

But there wasn't anybody else. He was all on his own, and he hated it.

Chapter Two

"I think it's a great idea, Caitlin. The thing is, I don't see when we're going to be able to get there…" Caitlin's dad looked at her apologetically. "I've got to help your gran this weekend – she wants her kitchen painted – and your mum's working."

"Oh…" Caitlin stirred her cereal. She really wanted to go and visit the shelter – of course they had a website, but it wasn't quite the same. She wanted her speech for the class to be good and it wouldn't be if she hadn't actually seen the place that she was talking about. She wanted to take photos too. She had her camera and she could print them out and hold them up for everyone to see.

"I'll do it." Aidan shoved his plate in the dishwasher and grabbed his bag. "See you later." He had to leave for school earlier than Caitlin as the secondary school was a lot further away.

"Hey, wait! What?" Caitlin yelped.

"I'll take you there. Tomorrow. We can go on our bikes, OK? Sounds fun. But it's Saturday so it'll have to be after football training."

He disappeared into the hallway, leaving Caitlin staring after him, until she suddenly remembered to yell, "Thanks, Aidan!" as he was going out of the front door.

"Aidan doesn't even like dogs or cats!" Caitlin said to Dad in surprise as the door slammed.

"It's not that he doesn't like them." Her dad shook his head. "It's just he always had small pets. They're easier to look after. It was too much for us to have a dog or a cat in the house when you were little."

Caitlin nodded thoughtfully. Aidan had two big cages in his bedroom now – one for his elderly rat, Trevor, and one for a whole tribe of gerbils. He loved them and Caitlin thought they were quite cute, just a bit too wriggly.

You couldn't really cuddle with a gerbil, she thought. Not like Ollie yesterday. He'd snuggled up on her lap while she watched a Disney film with Alice and he'd even purred. She smiled to herself. If they went to the shelter, maybe there would be some more kittens there? A gorgeous fluffy kitten, just like Ollie, who really needed a home…

"Hi, Caitlin! And this is Aidan, right? Your mum rang to say you'd be coming. I'm Anna, one of the volunteers. I'm hoping to train as a vet, so I help out here at the weekends and Lucy asked me to show you around. Lucy's the manager, the lady your mum spoke to."

Caitlin nodded and held up her camera. "That's really nice of you. Is it OK if I take some photos?" she asked nervously.

She'd been looking forward to coming to the shelter ever since Aidan had agreed to take her, but this morning she'd suddenly realized it would mean lots of talking to people that she didn't know, which wasn't her favourite thing.

"Sure! So Lucy said you're doing a
school project?"

"Yes. It's for our school's
Community Week. We raise money
for a charity by doing cake sales and
things. And this year everyone gets to
help choose what that is – we all have
to make a presentation about a charity
we think the school should help. My
auntie said you were trying to raise

money to build new pens?"

"That's right, for the dogs. We're getting so many, we need more room for them." She sighed. "Actually, we could do with more room full stop. We only have a small yard to exercise them in too. So … what would you like to start with? Cats or dogs?"

"Cats," Caitlin said eagerly. She'd never been desperate for a pet of her own, but after seeing Ollie she was starting to change her mind. He was so cute. And Dad had said they hadn't had a dog or a cat because she had been little, and she wasn't little any more…

The cat pens were cleverly designed, built so they could be opened up into a little outdoor area, and with shelves for the cats to sleep on. Anna explained that most cats liked being high up, it made them feel safe. They weren't really keen on sleeping on the floor. Caitlin and Aidan ooohed and ahhhed at all the kittens – especially a gorgeous ginger pair – but there were loads more fully grown cats. A lot of them had come to the shelter because their owners had been elderly and had moved into places they couldn't take cats, Anna told them. It was so sad.

"Shall we go and see the dogs now?" Anna suggested, and Caitlin jumped up. She'd been crouching by the last of the cat pens, trying to coax a sleepy tabby to come and be stroked, but the cat only yawned and flicked her ears.

"Oh! Yes please. I've already got lots of great photos for my school project though. Are you sure you're not supposed to be doing something else?"

Anna smiled. "No, it's OK. I do whatever needs doing. I'd rather show you two around than scrub water bowls!"

Caitlin looked back regretfully at the ginger kittens and followed Anna through a heavy door. She supposed that the shelter had to keep the dogs and cats properly separated so they didn't upset each other.

The dogs' section of the shelter felt completely different – it was so much noisier! The barking and whining started as soon as the dogs heard the door open, and Caitlin jumped.

"They're loud, aren't they?" Anna grinned at her. "It's hard for them being shut in so much of the time. One of the other jobs I do is take out a couple of dogs at a time to the park round the corner. It makes a big difference if they can get a good walk."

"There are so many…" Caitlin murmured, looking down the long passage lined with pens.

"And all of these are full?" Aidan asked.

"Yup." Anna sighed, leading the way

down the passage as the dogs whined and barked to be noticed. There were dogs pawing eagerly at almost every door. "We have to turn animals away sometimes, when we haven't got any more room."

Aidan nodded and then he brightened up, crouching to peer into one of the pens. "Hey, Caitlin, look!"

Caitlin leaned over his shoulder, peering at the dog inside. He was a lot smaller than most of the others – still a puppy, she realized.

"He's really cute, isn't he?" Aidan said, laughing as the little dog scrabbled eagerly at the wire of his door.

"That's Winston." Anna came over to see who they were looking at.

"He's a whippet crossed with we're not sure what. Maybe a Jack Russell – he's got a Jack Russell-ish tail. Isn't he gorgeous?"

"He's such a pretty colour," Caitlin said admiringly. "I've never seen a dog like that before! He's stripey!" She crouched down next to Aidan, and the puppy pressed his nose up against the wire door and tried to lick their faces. He was a lovely soft blue-grey colour, with peachy stripes and a white chest and paws. His fur was very smooth, except for the brush-like tail.

"I think the stripes are the whippet in him," Anna explained. "They come in brindle stripes like that quite often. Do you want to meet him properly? I can open the pen for you."

"Oh, yes please!" Caitlin wriggled back so Anna could open the door, and the excited puppy bounced all over her and Aidan, wriggling and licking and whining.

"His fur's almost silky," Caitlin said, running her hand over his smooth back. "It's so short and fine."

"One of the other volunteers is knitting him a jumper." Anna leaned down to stroke Winston too. "Seriously!" she added when Aidan pulled a face. "He needs one. Whippets get cold easily because they're so skinny and their fur's thin. She's trying to make him one that matches his stripes, a sort of blue-grey camo pattern."

"How old is he?" Caitlin asked. "He looks so little."

"About three months." Anna tickled the puppy under his chin, looking sad. "Someone left him and the rest of the litter outside the police station in a box and one of the police constables brought them round to us."

Caitlin stared at her in shock. "Who would do something like that?"

Anna shrugged. "I don't know. I suppose they didn't want puppies. Winston's two sisters went to new homes last week and he's missing them like crazy. He cries every time someone goes past."

"Ohhh…" Caitlin gulped. She could imagine how sad the beautiful little dog must be, left on his own.

The puppy looked up at her and stopped bouncing about. Instead, he gazed at Caitlin with his head on one side and put one small white paw on her knee, as if to tell her that it was all right. *He* was all right.

"You're such a sweetheart," Caitlin whispered. "I can't believe someone dumped you in a box. I came here thinking I might meet a gorgeous kitten, but you're even cuter than the cats. I'd look after you so well, if you were mine…"

Chapter Three

"Oh, he's adorable!" Caitlin's mum leaned over the table where Caitlin had laid out her photos. "Look at those big brown eyes!"

"I know! And the way his ears fold over. He's my favourite, he's called Winston. I took loads of pictures of him. I think I might make him the star of my project. Wouldn't you want to choose the Garland Animal Shelter as your school charity if you saw a photo of him? And if you heard that he'd been abandoned in a cardboard box?"

"Was he really?" Caitlin's mum looked shocked. "But he's so sweet!"

"Just wait till he's got a woolly jumper on," Aidan put in, picking up another photo of Winston. "Caitlin, did you take photos of any of the other dogs?"

"Yes! I didn't print out as many, that's all… Mum, can I go to the shelter again?"

Her mum looked surprised. "But you've got plenty of pictures already. You can't need any more than this, can you?"

"No… I didn't mean for the project. But the girl who showed us round, Anna, she was a volunteer. She said one of the things she does is take out the dogs for walks in the park. And I was thinking, maybe I could do that?"

"That's a nice thought, Caitlin, but I expect you need to be a bit older," her mum said, shaking her head.

"I'm nearly ten, Mum! It's my birthday in two weeks," Caitlin pointed out.

"Actually, Anna said there are some children who walk the dogs. But not on their own, they have to go with another volunteer." Aidan picked up a photo of Winston. "I think she said something about getting a form filled in by your parents. Caitlin was probably too busy falling in love with this puppy to notice."

Caitlin squeaked and threw her arms round him. "I didn't hear you talking to her about that! You're so clever!"

Aidan patted her on the head, which usually made Caitlin furious, but she'd forgive him anything right this minute. "Like I said, it was when you were cuddling Winston – you wouldn't have noticed if I'd yelled in your ear! It's OK, Mum, it's not far over to Garland Park on a bike and there's a cycle path most of the way. I don't mind going with Caitlin the first time maybe? There were some really cool dogs there, it'd be fun to walk them. And she could probably go on her own once she knows the way."

He dug a crumpled piece of paper out of his pocket and handed it to their mum. "Forms. Anna gave me them, I forgot. There you go."

"Can we go tomorrow?" Caitlin looked pleadingly at her mum. "If I finish doing my homework first?"

Caitlin spent the evening making a huge display board all about the shelter, with photos of the dogs and cats, and the small space that the dogs had to run around in. Even if she couldn't convince her class to choose the shelter as their charity, which she supposed wasn't all that likely, she definitely wanted to do something to help.

The photo in the middle of the board was of Winston, the one her mum had liked where his eyes were so big, and he looked so sad and cute.

After all the time she'd spent looking at photos of the little whippet, Caitlin couldn't wait to see him again for real. She even took Aidan a bacon sandwich in bed on Sunday morning, to try and persuade him that it was time to get up. But he ate the sandwich in about three bites, handed her back the plate and pulled the duvet over his head.

It was more than an hour later that her brother finally surfaced and he insisted on eating a second breakfast before they left. Caitlin couldn't eat. She was too excited. She sat there watching every mouthful of toast until Aidan groaned and finally gave up.

"I can't eat with you staring at me like that," he muttered. "Come on, then. I'll text Dad and tell him we're going

now and we'll be back for lunch, OK?
Go and get your bike."

Caitlin didn't think she'd ever cycled
so fast and Aidan was right – the
shelter wasn't far. She could definitely
do the ride on her own if Mum and
Dad would let her.

She hurried into the shelter, clutching the forms worriedly. What if they said she was too young? It would be awful. But Anna was there and she laughed.

"Look, Lucy, I told you she'd be back!"

"We've got the forms you gave Aidan," Caitlin said, her voice not much more than a whisper. She held them out to Lucy. "Um. Is it OK if we help out a bit? Can we walk the dogs?"

Aidan came in from locking up the bikes and Lucy smiled at them both. "Of course you can." She scanned down the form. "Yes, we've got all your contact numbers and this looks fine. There are a few health and safety rules we need to explain before we can let you go out, though. For a start you'll only be able to walk the smaller dogs, Caitlin – a lot of our dogs aren't used to walking nicely on a lead, so it can be quite hard work. But we'll send you out with an adult volunteer too."

Caitlin nodded. She'd sort of expected that – they weren't going to let her take a huge great Labrador out to the park on her own.

"And sometimes we need people to stay here as well," Lucy added. "Even playing with the dogs in the yard can be really helpful."

"We don't mind what we do, do we?" Aidan said, looking at Caitlin. "And we can help with the cats too – Anna said you need people to groom them."

"Yes, and to spend time with the younger ones," Lucy agreed. "Great. OK. I'll tell you what, Anna, why don't you take Aidan and Caitlin and a few of the younger dogs out into the yard for a bit first? The proper name for this is socialization," she added, "but it basically means showing them how to have fun."

Caitlin nodded eagerly. It sounded like the best possible job to her – spending the morning playing with dogs. She wasn't quite brave enough to ask if Winston was going to be one of the younger dogs that Lucy meant. After all, she wasn't volunteering only for him…

There was a door opening. Winston bounced up hopefully, his thin tail whipping from side to side. Were they coming for him? Could he go out? He scrabbled hopefully at the wire, standing up on his hind legs and whining.

No. They were only walking past him. Winston dropped down on to all four paws and stood watching mournfully as they went on down the passage and started to open up other doors. They were putting leads on the dogs. So they were going out.

Winston's tail drooped as he slunk back on to his cushion and slumped down with his chin on his paws.

Then one of his flopped-over ears twitched and he peered sideways from his cushion. Was that someone coming back? There were footsteps coming closer. He tensed up, ready to spring to the door, hoping they wouldn't just go past again…

The door of his pen rattled and he bounced up, whimpering with excitement. Yes! His door was opening! Winston whirled round the pen, barking and yipping and dancing in circles. A walk – he was actually getting to go outside!

He sort of knew that he needed to keep still long enough for them to clip the lead on to his collar, but he was too excited. He kept on barking and dancing until eventually the smaller girl knelt down and caught him so the older one could put his lead on. He nuzzled at the smaller girl, licking her cheek and feeling her laugh. He wriggled so much that he scrambled himself into her lap and felt her arms go round him, warm and tight.

Chapter Four

Caitlin giggled as Winston danced around her feet, bouncing excitedly on the end of his lead.

"How do you ever get him to walk anywhere?" Aidan asked Anna. He was holding on to a small brown terrier called Billy and Billy was watching Winston with his ears flattened back as if he was horrified.

"He's better when he gets outside, and there's stuff to look at and sniff. Actually, once he's fully grown he'll probably be able to run really fast. Whippets are great runners – they're like greyhounds but smaller."

"I looked them up," Caitlin admitted. "One of the websites said that if you let them off the lead they can disappear and you've got no hope of catching them."

"Exactly. Winston might not be as bad, because he's only half whippet, but we'd still say to his new owners that he's best kept on a lead until he's really well trained. Right, look, here's the yard. We can let them off in here because it's all closed in, but we've got to watch to make sure they're getting on OK."

Anna pulled open a door that led out to a small fenced area of scruffy grass, scattered with chewed rubber balls and rope toys. Then she crouched down and undid the lead on Pickle, the fluffy white Westie she'd brought out.

The two older dogs nosed cautiously on to the grass, but Winston bounced past them as soon as Caitlin undid his lead. He shot across the yard, ignoring the toys that Billy and Pickle started to nose at, and leaped about wildly.

"He really does love being outside!" Caitlin said to Anna, watching him bound around.

"He could do with a bigger space, to be honest," Anna said. "He's only a puppy, but see how strong his back legs are already?"

Caitlin nodded and then giggled as Winston came racing back towards them. He looked like he was running straight for her and Anna, as though he was going to crash right into them, but at the last second he swerved aside, jumping up to lick at Caitlin's arm.

"He's so cheeky!" Anna shook her head. "He seems to really like you too. Maybe if you came after school one

day this week, Lucy would let you take
him out to the park? He could have
more of a run then. He doesn't need
that much exercise now because he's so
little, but he loved it when I took him
there the other day."

Caitlin nodded, her eyes shining.
Anna thought that Winston liked
her! She watched as he dashed over
to the other end of the yard and then
she crouched down, patting her knees
hopefully. Would he understand what

she meant? Would he even want to come?

But the little brindle dog came hurtling back down the yard and flung himself at her, making excited *roo, roo* sort of noises that Caitlin had never heard from any dog before.

"Yes, you're so lovely, aren't you?" she said, giggling as he licked her ears and then jumped down to wriggle on his back on the grass, waving his paws in the air and still singing with happiness.

Aidan came to stand next to her,

shaking his head. "Caitlin, what did you *do* to that dog?"

Caitlin's mum dropped her off at the shelter on Tuesday afternoon – she'd wanted to go on Monday, but she had a swimming lesson. Caitlin had been hoping to walk Winston, but she didn't feel brave enough to ask Lucy. She'd do it next time, she promised herself. Instead she got to take Pickle out to the park with Christine, one of the older volunteers. She did say hello to Winston on the way to find Pickle, though.

"I've been coming here to help out for years," Christine explained. "I live in a flat where I can't have my own dog, so

I love getting the chance to spend time with the dogs at the shelter."

"Don't you miss them?" Caitlin asked her, after a while. "When they get rehomed, I mean?" She'd been a bit shy about talking to Christine at first, but then the big husky that Christine was walking had looped his lead around Christine's feet and tripped her up. By the time Caitlin had hauled her up again and helped brush the mud off her coat, a lot of the shyness had gone.

"Of course. But then you have to think of the homes they've gone to and how happy they are now. People send us photos sometimes too, that's always nice." Christine looked at her, smiling. "I know which one you're thinking of. That little whippet cross. Winston.

He's gorgeous, isn't he?"

Caitlin stared at her in surprise.

"You spent a good ten minutes talking to him through his pen door when you first arrived! I tell you what, shall we take these two back – I think Pickle's had enough anyway – and see if Lucy thinks Winston would like a run? I bet Millie would love a walk too, she's the Labrador cross in the pen by the door."

Walking Winston was even more fun than playing with him in the yard. Caitlin hadn't realized quite how fast he could be. She had to run too, since she couldn't let him off the lead, and she chased after him, panting and laughing. Luckily Winston ran about three times as far as she did, dashing backwards and forwards.

"Maybe he needs one of those extending leads," Christine said, when she caught up with them and saw Caitlin panting, with her hands on her knees, and Winston looking up at her impatiently.

"No!" Caitlin squeaked. Then she went pink. "Sorry… It's just … I read about those on a dog website. They're dangerous for whippets because they go so fast. If they pull the lead all the way out and then it stops them suddenly, it can hurt their necks really badly. They're supposed to have a long lead that you hold in loops. Or if you really want to use an extending lead, you need to use it with a harness, not a collar. One that goes round his middle." Caitlin held her hands round Winston's tiny shoulders, trying to show Christine what she meant, and Christine grinned at her.

"I didn't know that. You've been doing a lot of research."

Caitlin went even pinker. "I had to, for my school project," she explained.

"Not because you've fallen in love with a whippet?"

"Maybe a bit." Caitlin sighed. After swimming last night she'd spent ages on her mum's laptop, looking up whippets.

It seemed like the funny noises Winston made were a whippet thing – there were even videos online of whippet owners getting their dogs to "sing" on command. And so many photos of whippets on sofas and whippets sneaking on to people's beds!

Caitlin could imagine Winston climbing on to her bed, and getting under the duvet. Whippets had to have blankets to snuggle in, lots of the websites said so. It was because they were so skinny, it was hard for them to keep warm. Even though Winston was only half whippet, he was definitely a skinny little thing.

"So when do you have to speak to everybody at school about the shelter?" Christine asked. "You sounded a bit nervous about it when you were telling me earlier."

"Next Monday." Caitlin gave a little shudder. "My friend Lily's really excited about it – she's like that. She loves standing up in front of everybody, but I hate it." She shook herself determinedly. "I don't care, though, I'm still going to do it. If my class chooses the shelter, it'll go on a list of seven for the head and the teachers to pick from. One from each class, you see? And the school does all sorts of stuff for the charity they choose – sponsored sleepovers and a car wash … and … and cake sales. Last year it was nearly a thousand pounds we raised! Wouldn't that buy at least a bit of a new dog block?"

Christine nodded. "Of course it would. It would be great to have some extra money coming in. But even what you've done this afternoon is a great help, you know. Pickle and Winston wouldn't have got a walk today if you hadn't come to the shelter."

"I suppose so." Caitlin reached down to rub Winston's silky whippet ears. "But maybe me and my friends could try and raise some money as well. I just wish there was something more that I could do."

Winston sat on the grass, eyes closed and his nose pointing to the sky. He loved having his ears rubbed. Caitlin

was pulling them gently through her
fingers now and she was giggling.
She seemed happy too. It was sunny
and warm, and he'd raced all over the
park with her – he'd run so fast he was
feeling quite worn out and relaxed
now, especially with all the fussing
over his ears. Winston
slumped
down,
his nose
resting on
his paws, and
groaned with sleepy happiness.

"He's purring!" Caitlin whispered.
"I didn't know dogs could purr!"

"Neither did I," said Christine,
laughing. "But it definitely sounds
like it."

Winston rolled over on to his back, waving his little white paws in the air, still purring.

"We've got to go back, Winston," Caitlin called gently. "Home time. Christine, I think he's asleep! We must have walked him for too long."

"I suppose he is only a puppy."

Winston hardly noticed when Caitlin picked him up. His eyelids flickered a little and then he snuggled closer in to her school skirt. His sleepy purr deepened to a little whippet snore.

Caitlin jumped carefully down from the branch of the big tree in the garden and looked up at the banner.

"It's a bit lopsided," Sean said, squinting at it, but Lily glared at him.

IN AID OF GARLAND ANIMAL SHELTER

"It's brilliant, Caitlin," she said. "Don't go back up in the tree, it's too wobbly, I kept thinking you were going to fall. And it doesn't matter if it's lopsided, everyone can see what it says."

Caitlin made a face. "At least you can read it. I had to squash up the 'shelter' because I was running out of space. Oh well."

"Can I buy this?" Alice asked hopefully, holding up a Barbie doll from one of the bags Lily had piled on the table.

"Have you got any money?" Caitlin asked, surprised.

"No… But only because Mum had run out of change so she couldn't give us our pocket money. I'll pay later," Alice promised.

"My mum thinks this is a brilliant idea," Lily told Caitlin. "I finally cleared out the cupboard in the corner of my room. And look what she sent." She fished around in another of her bags and opened up a big tin of flapjacks. "She said we can eat them or sell them, she doesn't mind."

"Sell them!" Caitlin said, at the same time as Alice and Sean said, "Eat them!"

"Oh, OK. You can have one each, but we'll sell the rest," Caitlin allowed.

She walked round the front of the table, looking at it admiringly. They'd put more printouts of the photos she'd taken along the front, and a description of the new space the shelter wanted to build for the dogs – she'd found that on the website. Mum had helped her make a batch of chocolate brownies, and Auntie Jen had sent Rice Krispie cakes with Alice and Sean.

Now all they needed were customers. The problem was, Caitlin's road wasn't all that busy. An hour later, Alice was sulking because Caitlin wouldn't let her eat any more cake and Sean had decided that most of the old toys he'd brought to sell he wanted back after all. They'd sold some chocolate brownies to Mrs Marsh who lived next door, but that was about it.

"How's it going?" Caitlin's mum

came out on to the front step.

Caitlin sighed and slumped down on the grass. "No one's going past. We made all the cakes and everything but we haven't got any customers."

"Oh dear… Never mind. I'm sure it'll get better."

Ten minutes later, Caitlin was starting to feel like giving up when Lily came running back down the road. She'd taken some flapjacks to see if she could sell them to one of her friends who lived in the next street. "Caitlin! Your brother's coming, with a whole load of people!"

Caitlin got up off the grass and ran to look where Lily was pointing.

"Where's he been?" Lily asked. "Who are they?"

"He went out to play football. That's everyone from his team!" Caitlin dashed back to stand behind the table. "And the team they were playing as well, by the looks of it. Mum must have called him! Put out all the cakes! Make it look nice!"

Caitlin didn't think the football team would want her old toys, or Lily's, but lots of them must have had little sisters. By the time they'd gone, there wasn't a crumb of cake left, and most of the toys had been sold too.

"We made thirty-five pounds!" Lily yelped, tipping the coins back into the ice-cream tub they'd been keeping the sales money in.

Caitlin hugged her and then hugged Aidan. "Thank you, thank you, thank you! I'm going to the shelter this afternoon – I can give them the money then."

Chapter Five

Miss Lewis beamed at Lily and wrote up the name of the riding stable on the whiteboard. "Well done, Lily, that was a great idea. OK… Caitlin, you're next."

Caitlin knew she was – they were going round table by table, so she had to be. She'd sat through Lily's talk with her heart thumping so hard it seemed to be blocking her throat and her hands were icy cold.

She wasn't entirely sure how she got to the front of the classroom, but she was there and everyone was staring at her. Caitlin stared back for what seemed like ages and then forced herself to look at the photo of Winston in the middle of her board. He was gazing back at her with huge dark eyes.

Caitlin took a deep breath. "My charity is the Garland Animal Shelter.

It's near here, over by Garland Park. They take in lots of dogs and cats every month and they always need more money. This is Winston…" She pointed to his picture. "He's only three months old – or about that. No one knows exactly because he was dumped outside the police station in a cardboard box…" She heard the gasp as she said it and everyone leaned forward to look at the photo, and then Miss Lewis had to tell the class to shush.

After that, the talk felt a lot easier, and Caitlin was almost surprised when she got to the end. It seemed to have gone a lot faster than when she had practised it with Dad. And everyone clapped!

"That was great, Caitlin, what a gorgeous dog. And cute kittens as well. OK, so just a couple more of you to go and then it's time for the voting. Lakshmi, it's your turn next."

"Well done!" Lily whispered. "I thought you said you were really nervous, you didn't sound it at all."

"I was!" Caitlin smiled at her in relief. "I had to keep looking at Winston to make me talk."

Lily sighed. "I'll have to come to the shelter and see him, he's so sweet."

There were twenty-seven different charities up on the board by the end of the morning. Miss Lewis said that they would do the actual voting after lunch, once they'd all had a chance to think about it.

"I'll vote for the shelter," Lily promised as she opened her lunch box. "I might have done even if we *were* allowed to vote for our own charity. I can't believe somebody left those puppies in a box."

"I will too." James leaned across the table. "And I'm going to get my mum and dad to look at the website. I've been asking them if we can have a dog for ages and they've sort of said yes. That puppy's so cute, he'd definitely persuade my mum. And I bet my dad would love him too."

Caitlin stared at him and tried to smile. Of course she wanted everyone in the class to vote for the shelter. And of course she wanted Winston to have a new home. But ... not just yet.

She and Christine were going to try and train Winston to walk to heel properly. She'd even found a pattern for a sort of whippet scarf and she'd been planning to get Mum to help her knit one. There wouldn't be time if Winston found a new home so quickly – she needed him to stay at the shelter a bit longer…

Caitlin swallowed hard. In fact, she didn't want Winston to go to a new owner at all.

"That's amazing, Caitlin." Lucy gave her a hug. "You should be really proud of yourself." She looked down at Caitlin and put her head on one side. "For someone who's just got the whole school to choose their favourite charity to support, you don't look that happy."

Caitlin looked down at her feet. "Everyone thought Winston was really cute when I showed them the photos yesterday," she explained. "James in my class, he's been trying to persuade his parents to get a dog. And he said he was going to show them Winston on the website. Then he came running up to me in the playground this morning and he says his mum's going to call you

today about coming to see Winston.
Sometime this weekend, probably."

"Ohhh… I see." Lucy hugged her
again. "It's the hardest thing about
volunteering here. Why do you think
I've got four cats at home?"

"Four?" Caitlin laughed and sniffed
at the same time.

"Yup. I couldn't resist… I'd have dogs
as well, except I'm not home enough.
And the cats would never forgive me."

Caitlin nodded. "My mum and dad
both work. Not always at the same time,
though. I'd started thinking, maybe we
could have a dog. A little dog, because
our house isn't massive. And me and
my brother could do the walking. I was
working my way up to talking to them
about it, but I was worried they'd say

no. We've always had small pets, you see – my dad's got fish, and my brother has gerbils and a rat." She sniffed again. "Now it's too late."

"I promise there'll be another dog you fall in love with," Lucy said gently. "And think how happy Winston will be with someone to give him all the attention he wants."

Caitlin nodded. Of course she wanted somebody to make Winston happy. But she wanted that person to be *her*.

"Are you going to be here at the weekend?" Lucy asked her. "I'm thinking about who's going to be around when, for exercising the dogs. Anna's here, but Christine's away."

"Mum says I can come on Saturday. Not Sunday though, it's my birthday."

"Oh, nice. Are you having a party?"

Caitlin shook her head. "I don't know. Mum's arranging it. My friend Lily's coming over and we're going somewhere special, but it's a surprise. Last year we went to the beach, it was brilliant. But Mum says the weather forecast's not that good this weekend."

And somehow, she just couldn't get excited about whatever it was they were going to do. She'd almost rather be at the shelter, spending precious time with Winston before he went. James and his family wouldn't be able to take Winston home with them, even if they came on Saturday, not until Lucy or one of the other staff had gone round to do a home check. She had just a little bit longer to wish he was hers.

Winston dashed down to the end of
the yard, chasing after the ball. He
shook it fiercely for a minute and then
hurried back to Caitlin.

"You're supposed to bring it to *me*,
silly." She rubbed his ears gently and
Winston leaned against her. Caitlin
wasn't running up and down with
him like she usually did, and
laughing. She was sitting on
the grass instead, with
one arm wrapped
round her knees,
and she kept
stroking
him, over
and over.

That was nice – he liked being stroked. But something seemed different. He rested his nose on her knee and stared up at her worriedly. Something wasn't right. *She* wasn't right.

"What's the matter, Winston? Look, here's another ball." Caitlin threw it down to the end of the yard, but Winston didn't chase after it. Instead he came round to the side of her and climbed determinedly into her lap, snuggling himself half inside her hoodie. She was warm, but that wasn't why. He wanted to be next to her.

She needed him.

Chapter Six

"Is that your friend from school?" Lucy murmured to Caitlin, as James and his family came up the front steps.

"Yes." Caitlin swallowed.

"Do you want to go and help with the cats?" Lucy suggested gently. "I know how you feel about Winston, you don't have to be around if it's going to make you sad."

Caitlin shook her head. "James knows I'm going to be here. It'd be weird if I didn't say hello."

"And Winston likes you," Lucy pointed out. "He'll probably be a bit less shy if you're around too. Hello! You're the Logans? You've come to look at Winston?"

Caitlin recognized James's mum from the school playground, and his younger sister was in the year below them at school. "Hi, James. Hi, Abbie."

"Caitlin volunteers at the shelter," Lucy explained.

"Yes, and it was Caitlin who showed James the photo of Winston," James's dad said, smiling at her. "He looks like the perfect dog for us, Caitlin. Thank you!"

Caitlin smiled at him, even though she didn't feel like it. She thought her smile probably looked a bit fake, but no one seemed to notice.

"Shall I get Winston out of his pen and bring him into the yard?" she suggested to Lucy. If people had asked to look at a particular dog, they got to spend some time with them in the yard or a little playroom indoors, to see if they all got on.

Caitlin hurried through to the pens

and undid Winston's door. Even though she was feeling so miserable, she still couldn't help laughing as he danced around her while she tried to put on his lead. She loved it that he was so excited.

"You're going to meet some really nice people," she whispered, as she finally managed to clip the lead on to his collar. "They might even take you home. I bet James would love it if you wanted to sleep on his bed. And they'll take you for so many walks. It's going to be brilliant. You might just have to learn to be nice to his cat, that's all," she added, remembering James talking about his cat and the guide dog puppies next door.

Caitlin led Winston out to the yard, where James and his family were waiting with Lucy.

"Oh, he's even cuter than his photos!" Abbie squeaked, and Caitlin felt Winston press himself against her leg nervously.

"It's OK," she murmured. "Come on, come and see." She coaxed Winston forward and he peered round her legs at the family, wagging his tail slowly.

"Aren't you beautiful?" James's dad said quietly, crouching down. "Gently, Abbie. Let him get used to us first."

"I read that whippets are touch-sensitive?" James's mum asked Lucy, sounding a little worried. "Do we need to be careful stroking him? We don't want to scare him."

Caitlin bit her bottom lip. James and Abbie were being so quiet and patient, and James's mum and dad sounded like they were going to be great dog owners. They'd been doing their research, just like she had. She'd been secretly hoping that James and his family would turn out not to be the right home for Winston, but they were perfect.

"As long as you're careful and he can see what you're doing, he won't startle. Do you want to take his lead?" Lucy suggested to James's dad, and Caitlin handed it over.

"I'll go and … and…" She didn't really know what she was going to do. Caitlin ducked back through the door into the main dog area. She just couldn't watch any more.

Winston turned to look as Caitlin slipped out of the door and pulled a little on his lead to follow her. There were other people round him now and he couldn't see where Caitlin had gone. He whined worriedly, not sure what was going on, but Lucy was there, murmuring gently to him and stroking his ears.

He liked Lucy. She brought his food most days and she always stopped to fuss over him. The people with her were talking to him and stroking him too. Perhaps it was all right that Caitlin wasn't there, but he wished she'd stayed. He liked the way she rubbed his ears best and the way she whispered to him. He was sure that Caitlin hadn't gone far. Maybe she was just beyond that door?

"Winston?" Lucy was calling to him, and he turned, letting her show him a ball so the children could throw it for him to chase. A run up and down the yard! That was what he wanted.

But it would have been better if Caitlin had stayed.

Caitlin leaned against the wall just inside the yard door. It wasn't completely shut, and she could hear Abbie and James laughing and talking to Winston. It sounded like he was totally failing to fetch a ball again. He just wasn't very good at it. He loved the racing about bit, though.

Probably she ought to go back out there and smile and be nice and tell James's family how gorgeous Winston was. As if they couldn't see that for themselves already. Or she should do what Lucy had suggested and go and help Anna feed the cats. Anything except stand here listening to the family falling in love with her gorgeous puppy. But she couldn't drag herself away.

Caitlin blinked, realizing that there was a change in the voices outside. They were quieter, more worried. Uncertainly, she moved closer to the door, wondering what was going on.

"And is he a fairly young cat?" Lucy was asking.

"Yes, that's my only worry about getting a dog," James's mum said. "Biscuit's a bit nervous. I don't want to upset him. That's one reason we wanted to get a puppy, you see. We thought an older dog might find it harder to accept living with a cat – but a puppy wouldn't know any different?"

Lucy was silent for a minute and Caitlin peeped round the door to see her. She was looking worried.

"Usually, I'd absolutely agree with you. Puppies do learn to live with cats, and it's not a problem for most dogs…"

"What's the matter?" James asked. "Doesn't Winston like cats?"

"To be honest, he's never really met one," Lucy said, smiling at him. "But it's his breed that's the problem. Because he's half whippet, and whippets are what are called sighthounds. That means they were bred to be hunting dogs and they hunted by sight, not smell. Winston's going to have whippet instincts. That means he's going to want to chase anything small and furry that's running away from him."

"Oh…" James's dad made a face. "That sounds like Biscuit…"

"I'm not saying that he would." Lucy frowned a little. "Just that he *might*. It's a risk. And for that reason, we'd never recommend rehoming a sighthound where there's already a cat in the family."

Caitlin turned back from the door and pressed her hand over her mouth. She was smiling an enormous smile and she knew she shouldn't be, but she couldn't help it…

Chapter Seven

"James's family are going to take Millie home instead," Caitlin told Winston, as she filled up his food bowl. "Her old owner had a cat, and she was really good and didn't chase him or anything like that. Lucy thinks she might miss him, actually." She watched Winston gobble down his food. "I bet you'd have loved living with James and Abbie.

They're nice. They'd have made such a big fuss of you. I wonder if you really would have chased their cat?" It was hard to imagine Winston being so fierce – he was such a sweet, friendly puppy. But Lucy had explained to her afterwards that it wasn't something he would decide to do – it was a hunting instinct and it had been part of whippets for centuries.

"Even if you're not going to be James's dog, you're going to get a new owner soon…" Caitlin crouched down, watching Winston wolf down his dog biscuits. "You're too beautiful to stay here for long – your sisters didn't, did they? And everyone in my class thought you were gorgeous." She sighed. "I have to get used to it. Lucy

says I'll fall in love with another dog
once you've gone…"

Winston glanced up from his bowl of
food and stared at her. He looked as if
he was outraged by the idea and Caitlin
giggled. "No, I don't think so either.
But someone's going to want to take
you home any day now." She shivered.
"It could even be tomorrow. Unless I
persuade Mum and Dad that we should
adopt you instead. And to be honest,
I can't see that working. Even though
they do keep saying how brilliant it is
that I'm helping at the shelter, I don't
think they really want a dog."

Caitlin sat down on the floor,
leaning against the wall of the pen.
"I probably ought to go and help feed
all the others. Lucy hasn't said it, but

it isn't fair if I keep making a big fuss over you. I've got to let you fall in love with a new owner." She rubbed the back of her arm across her eyes. "I just can't help thinking you'd be so much better off with me…"

Winston licked the last bits of dog biscuit out of his bowl and stared at it hopefully in case any more food suddenly arrived, but it didn't. He padded over to Caitlin and rested his nose on her knee.

"Perhaps I should get Mum and Dad to come and visit. Then maybe they'd want to take you home," Caitlin suggested, looking back into his soft dark eyes. "I don't see how anybody wouldn't want to. Unless they had a cat. And I suppose we'd have to be super-careful with Aidan's gerbils, and Trevor. But he keeps them in his room all the time anyway."

Caitlin ran her hand over Winston's smooth neck and her voice wobbled. "I can't bear thinking about you going somewhere else and forgetting all about me. Anna said this morning that you always look disappointed when she takes you out to the yard for exercise and I'm not there. I don't know if she was just being nice, but

I do think you're pleased to see me, aren't you?"

Winston leaned over to lick her hand and then he slumped down on the floor of the pen on his back, waving his legs in the air for Caitlin to rub his tummy.

"I can see your dinner! You go skinny little whippet, great big bulge, skinny little whippet."

Winston rolled over again and climbed into Caitlin's lap, snuggling up with a huge, happy sigh. Caitlin sat watching him as he wriggled himself comfy and closed his eyes and then she stroked him, over and over, loving his peachy stripes. She was trying to fix them in her mind, she realized, in case he was gone by the time she came back.

"Caitlin!"

"That's Mum," Caitlin whispered, trying to stand up without waking the puppy on her lap. "She said she'd come and pick me up. I'll see you on Tuesday." She swallowed hard. "At least … I hope I will."

Winston curled himself into a ball on Caitlin's lap. He was deliciously full and deliciously warm, and she was stroking him. He snoozed, making little whippet whining noises as he dreamed of running through the park and chasing squirrels.

He half woke as she stood up and gently laid him on his cushion. She even pulled a blanket up around him and tucked him in, so that he was cosy. But then the metal door of the pen clanged behind her and Winston woke up properly.

Caitlin was going! She was leaving him behind! He wanted her to stay, to snuggle up with him. Whimpering, he tried to wriggle his way out of the blanket, but it all got caught up around his paws. By the time he'd dragged himself up and across the pen, she was gone.

Winston sat down by his door, lifted his head, and wailed.

"Are you OK, Caitlin?" her mum asked, as they drove home. "You're ever so quiet. Usually you come home from the shelter telling me stories about all the things the dogs have done, or how you nearly lost a guinea pig behind a cupboard, or something..."

Caitlin leaned her head against the car window. "I'm just a bit tired."

"So Lucy said that James's family can't take Winston after all? That's sad."

"Yes," Caitlin agreed, even though she didn't think it was. "But she says she's sure someone will adopt him soon."

"You should have taken me to see him," her mum said, glancing sideways.

"We weren't in a hurry. I'd love to meet him, now you've told me so much about him."

"Mum, have you ever wanted to have a dog?" Caitlin asked suddenly.

"Ummm." Her mum was silent for a minute, looking at the road. "We've always been a bit busy just with you and Aidan. It isn't that I *don't* want a dog, I've just never felt desperate for one, do you know what I mean?"

"Yes…" Caitlin sighed. It wasn't enough. Her mum and dad would have to pay for food and vet bills and special fleecy harnesses that didn't rub a whippet's skin. They'd have to take Winston for walks and arrange for him to be looked after when they went on holiday. It was no good her mum just not *not* wanting one. Everyone in her family needed to be enthusiastic about getting a dog. Caitlin turned back to the window, so her mum couldn't see the tears spilling down her cheeks.

Chapter Eight

Usually Caitlin woke up on her
birthday feeling excited. Last year, when
she couldn't think what sort of party
she'd like to have, her dad had organized
a surprise trip for the four of them
and Lily. Caitlin had woken up at six,
desperate to find out where they were
going. She'd loved it so much, she'd
asked for another surprise this year.

But today she couldn't feel happy. She wasn't looking forward to the trip at all. Would it be really ungrateful to say she didn't want a birthday treat, she'd rather go to the shelter?

Caitlin sighed and huddled her duvet up over her head. Of course it would. Mum and Dad had planned whatever it was, and they'd arranged for Lily to come over. She couldn't get out of it, however much she wanted to. She wondered vaguely what they had planned. Mum was right, it definitely wasn't good enough weather for a beach trip, like last year. That had been such a brilliant day – they'd swum and splashed in the sea, and built sandcastles, and buried her dad in the sand.

Of course, it would have been

even better if they'd had a dog. Did Winston like to dig, Caitlin wondered. She could just imagine him spraying sand everywhere and sneezing as he got it all up his nose. He probably wouldn't want to swim, she thought, because it would be too cold for him. And one of the websites she'd read said that swimming was harder for whippets because they were so slim, they didn't have any fat to help them float. But maybe he'd like to paddle…

"Are you are awake under there?"

Caitlin burrowed out from under her duvet to see her mum looking round the door. "Mmm…"

"Happy birthday, sweetheart. Are you coming to have breakfast? I've got those waffles you really like."

Caitlin nodded. She knew she ought to be leaping out of bed and racing downstairs, but she didn't feel bouncy and birthday-ish at all. "I'll be down in a minute," she told her mum.

Mum and Dad and Aidan were all sitting round the kitchen table, which was heaped with a pile of birthday cards and parcels. And even though Caitlin wasn't in a birthday mood, the parcels did look quite exciting.

"Now, these are from Gran, and Nanny and Grandad," her mum explained. "And there are a couple of little ones from us. But you'll have to wait till later for the rest of your presents."

Caitlin blinked at her, confused. "Why?"

"You'll see what I mean, I promise." Her mum smiled.

"OK…" Caitlin nodded and started to open the stack of cards. There wasn't a present from Auntie Jen and Alice and Sam, which was odd. They always sent something. Maybe they were coming over to give it to her instead.

"Oh, Lily's here." Caitlin's dad jumped up as the doorbell rang and Caitlin heard him murmuring to Lily's mum in the hallway. Lily came dashing into the kitchen and gave her a hug.

"Hello! Happy birthday! Did you get any good presents? I've got you one, but you can't open it now – you have to wait till later."

Caitlin turned to look accusingly at her mum, and her dad who'd followed Lily back into the kitchen.

"Are my presents something to do

113

with my birthday trip?" she asked. "Where are we going? This is really weird…"

"Don't worry. It's worth the wait." Aidan stuffed half a waffle in his mouth and then talked through it. "You're going to love it. Promise."

Caitlin passed the plate of waffles to Lily and nibbled on the edge of hers – they were her favourite breakfast food, but today she wasn't feeling that hungry. And even though she was still feeling sad about Winston, she couldn't help being curious about where they were going. Everyone else seemed so excited. Lily wouldn't stop giggling to herself, and her mum and dad kept giving each other conspiratorial looks.

"You have to tell me what's going

on!" she burst out.

"Not a chance," her dad said, grinning. "But it is time to go. Aidan, have you got the blindfold?"

"A blindfold?" Caitlin squeaked. "Why?"

Aidan made a *duh*! noise. "So you can't see where we're going?"

"You can't be mean to her, it's her birthday," Lily said sternly. "Put it on, Caitlin, we want to go!"

"OK…" Caitlin muttered. "This is so strange." But she stood up and let Aidan wrap one of her mum's scarves round her eyes.

"How many fingers am I holding up?"

"I don't *know!*"

"All right. She can't see. Lily, you take her other arm. Come on, Caitlin."

Caitlin felt them grab her arms and she stumbled down the hallway and out of the front of the house. Somebody unlocked the car – she heard it bleep. "So we're going in the car?" she asked. She wasn't sure if she was excited or nervous, her stomach had gone wobbly.

"Don't bang your head on the door," Lily said. "Duck down a bit. This is so funny, Caitlin. It's the best birthday surprise ever, I promise."

"Are we going a long way?" Caitlin asked, as she fumbled with her seat belt. She was in the middle, between Lily and Aidan.

"Ummm…" Lily sounded doubtful.

"No more questions," Caitlin's mum said firmly. "We don't want you guessing, it's got to be a surprise."

Caitlin leaned back against the car seat, biting her bottom lip. It felt so weird, driving without being able to see where they were going. She was almost shocked when the car stopped a few minutes later, and she could hear Aidan and Lily clicking their seat belts undone. "Are we here?" she murmured, turning her head from side to side, trying to work out where they might be. They'd gone about as far as her school, she reckoned, but that didn't make sense.

"Yup. Here, come this way." Aidan pulled her gently, and Caitlin climbed out of the car and stood waiting. There weren't any clues to where she was – the only sounds were cars going by. They could be anywhere.

"Up the steps," her dad said, and she felt his arm round her shoulders, leading her forwards. Someone opened a door – Caitlin could hear its squeaky *whoosh* noise – and then she knew where they were.

She could smell it. The special disinfectant they used to clean up – and now that she'd worked it out, she could hear barking as well, very quiet barking, muffled by the doors to the dog pens.

They were at the shelter.

Caitlin turned, grabbing at her dad's arm. "Dad? What are we doing here?"

Lucy laughed – Caitlin was sure it was her. She guessed Lucy must be standing behind the reception desk. "I told you she'd know as soon as she arrived!"

"Awww, I was hoping we'd get you as far as the pen," Caitlin's mum said. "You can take the blindfold off now, sweetheart."

Caitlin reached up to pull it off and looked around at them all. Everyone was beaming at her, but she couldn't see why. Or why they'd brought her here.

"You still haven't worked it out, have you?" said Aidan with a huge grin.

"No..."

"We were going to take you and Lily ice skating," her mum explained. "But then we changed our minds. Look." She nodded towards the door that led through to the dog pens and Anna, who was pushing it open with her shoulder. Her hands were full with a small blue-grey striped dog, a dog who had started to make silly, happy yipping noises as soon as he saw Caitlin.

"Now, just bear in mind that Winston is absolutely not your birthday present, as it's not a good idea to give pets as presents, and he's going to belong to the whole family…" Dad explained.

"But his collar and lead and the basket and blankets and bowls and toys and the massive book about whippets Dad found – all of that is your birthday present," Aidan put in.

"And I bought you a brilliant T-shirt with a whippet on it," Lily said. "Me and Mum found it yesterday. I wanted you to be wearing it when you got him, but I thought you might guess. And if you didn't guess it would make you miserable again."

"Miserable?" Caitlin asked, blinking as Anna gently put Winston into her arms and he wriggled, trying to lick her all over.

"You've been miserable all week, Caitlin! Even when Mr Turner was telling everybody in assembly that the school was going to support the shelter and help build new pens for more dogs, you looked like a wet weekend! It's been ever since James said he wanted to adopt Winston. I told your mum in the playground, when you forgot your homework book on Wednesday."

Caitlin turned round to stare at her mum over Winston's head.

"We'd already been so impressed by everything you were doing, Caitlin. You were working so hard, coming here after school and then doing your garden sale. Aidan said you were desperate for a dog. I rang the shelter to ask if someone could do a home check for us that weekend, you know. And then Lily told me how much you loved Winston – but when I spoke to Lucy, James's family had already arranged to come and see him. I couldn't believe I was too late."

"I rang your mum as soon as we realized they wouldn't be able to take Winston because of their cat," Lucy told her, smiling. "She and your dad came in to see him last night."

"When we left you with Aidan because we said we had a couple of special last-minute birthday things to get," her dad explained, "we were here. And then we went to the big pet store outside town."

"But ... but I didn't think you

wanted a dog! Mum, you said, in the car yesterday!"

"Yes, well, I couldn't exactly say, yes I'd love a dog and actually we're getting a gorgeous whippet, could I?" Caitlin's mum came to put her arms round her and Winston, and laughed as the puppy scrambled up to lick her too. "I had to pretend and it was very difficult. I wanted to tell you so much, especially when I could see how sad you were! I nearly gave in and blurted it out, but I thought Dad and Aidan and Lily would never forgive me."

"I still can't believe it," Caitlin murmured. "We've really got a dog!" It was hard to think of anything with a whippet puppy licking her all over. "Oooh, not in my ear!"

Winston wriggled out from underneath the blanket again and padded across the floor to Caitlin. He didn't want to stay in the basket, even though it was comfortable. If he went to sleep in there, she'd be gone when he woke up, he was sure.

He grabbed the blanket in his teeth and yanked at it, pulling it out so it trailed after him as he pattered across to her.

"Hey, didn't you like it in there? I was only getting a drink."

Winston dropped the blanket on her foot and then lay down. He wasn't really sure about this new place and the basket, but Caitlin was the same

and he wasn't letting her get away
this time. He twitched at the blanket,
trying to pull it so it covered him, but
Caitlin reached down and scooped him
up inside it. Then she sat down next
to his basket on the floor, with him on
her lap. Winston sniffed suspiciously
at the basket and then turned round a
few times until he was comfortable. He
rested his nose on her arm so that she
couldn't move.

"It's OK," Caitlin whispered, pulling
the blanket a little tighter around her
puppy. "I'm not going anywhere. And
you're staying, I promise."

Winston's ears flickered, but he was
already half asleep.

HOLLY WEBB

Holly Webb started out as a children's
book editor and wrote her first series for
the publisher she worked for. She has been
writing ever since, with over one hundred
books to her name. Holly lives in Berkshire,
with her husband and three young sons.
Holly's pet cats are always nosying around
when she is trying to type on her laptop.

For more information
about Holly Webb visit:

www.holly-webb.com